D1178898

This edition published by Parragon Books Ltd in 2014

Parragon Books Ltd
Chartist House
15–17 Trim Street
Bath BA1 1HA, UK
www.parragon.com

Copyright © 2014 Disney Enterprises, Inc.

All rights reserved. No part of this publication may be reproduced, stored in a retrieval
system or transmitted, in any form or by any means, electronic, mechanical, photocopying,
recording or otherwise, without the prior permission of the copyright holder.

ISBN 978-1-4723-6954-3

Printed in China

Bath • New York • Cologne • Melbourne • Delhi
Hong Kong • Shenzhen • Singapore • Amsterdam

The kingdom of Arendelle was a busy and happy place, nestled among the mountains of the far north. At night, the colourful northern lights often lit up the sky in beautiful patterns.

A kind king and queen ruled Arendelle. Their young daughters, Elsa and Anna, were the joy of their lives. But the royal couple had a secret worry....

Their eldest daughter,
Elsa, had a magical power.
She could create snow and
freeze things with her hands!

Anna, the younger daughter, adored her big sister.
The two were inseparable. One night, Anna convinced
Elsa to sneak into the Great Hall in the castle and
create a winter wonderland!

But while the girls were playing, Elsa accidentally hit Anna with a blast of icy magic. Little Anna fell to the ground, shivering. A streak of white appeared in her hair. Frightened for her sister, Elsa called out for help.

The worried king and queen rushed their daughters to the realm of trolls. The trolls were mysterious healers who knew about magic.

A wise old troll spoke to them. "You are lucky it wasn't her heart that was struck," he said. "The heart is not so easily changed, but the head can be persuaded. We should remove all magic, even memories of magic, to be safe."

The old troll was able to cure Anna by changing her memories, removing all magic from her mind. This meant she wouldn't remember Elsa's magical power.

The troll warned the king and queen: "Fear will be your enemy."

Back in Arendelle, the king and queen felt more worried than ever. They locked the castle gates and taught Elsa to control her powers so that no one would find out about them. But whenever she had strong feelings, the magic spilled out. So the king gave her a pair of gloves to help hold it back.

Elsa decided that to keep Anna safe, it would be best to stay away from her.

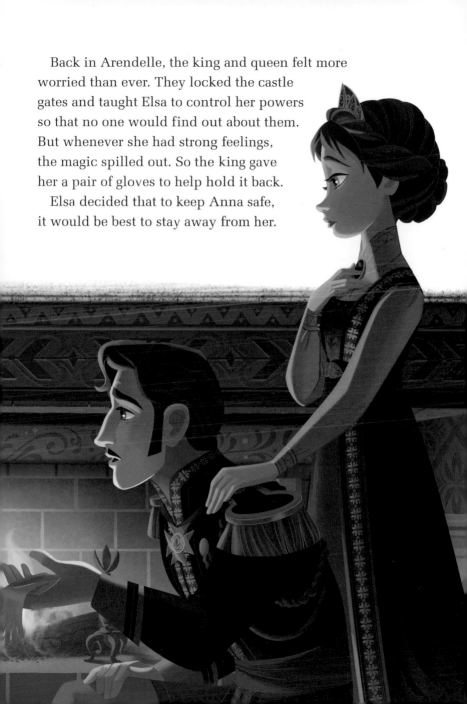

As the girls grew, Anna kept trying to spend time with
her sister. But Elsa always said that she was busy –
she was afraid that she might hurt Anna again.

As the years passed, the girls became more and
more like strangers. Then, when the two were
teenagers, the king and queen were tragically lost
in a storm at sea. The sisters felt sadder and more
alone than ever.

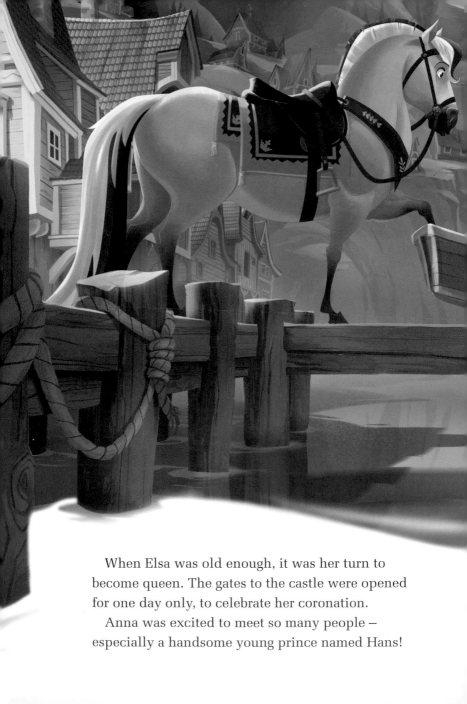

When Elsa was old enough, it was her turn to become queen. The gates to the castle were opened for one day only, to celebrate her coronation.

Anna was excited to meet so many people — especially a handsome young prince named Hans!

But Elsa was still struggling to hide her powers. She just hoped that she could make it through the day without anybody finding out about them.

To Elsa's relief, the celebration went exactly as planned. Everybody cheered for their beautiful new queen.

Afterwards, a party was held in the Great Hall. Anna and Prince Hans spent the evening laughing, dancing and talking. They had so much in common! Everything seemed perfect, so they made a big decision....

Anna introduced Hans to Elsa – and announced that they were going to be married.

Elsa was shocked. "You can't marry a man you just met," she told Anna.

"You can if it's true love," Anna insisted.

But Elsa would not listen to Anna's arguments. "My answer is no," she said firmly. "The party is over!"

Elsa started to leave the room, but Anna grabbed her hand – she was trying to make Elsa stay and talk. But Anna accidentally pulled off her sister's glove!

Anna kept arguing. She was confused and angry. "Why do you shut me out?" she asked Elsa. "I can't live like this anymore!"

"Enough!" Elsa cried. An icy blast
shot from her uncovered hand,
sending a sheet of ice across
the ballroom! Everyone
stared in disbelief.

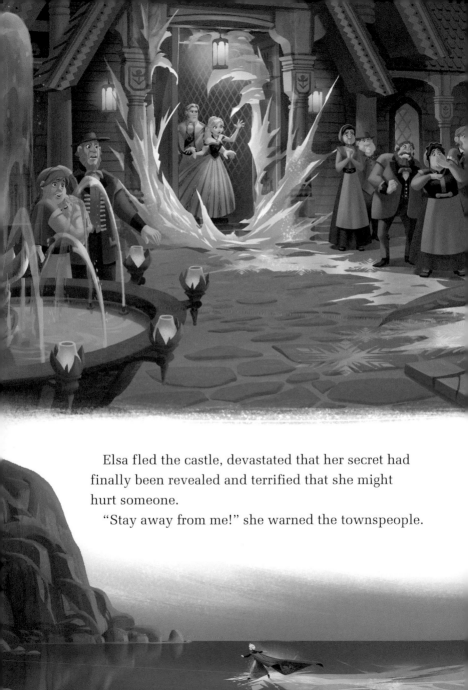

Elsa fled the castle, devastated that her secret had finally been revealed and terrified that she might hurt someone.

"Stay away from me!" she warned the townspeople.

Everything around Elsa turned to ice as she ran.
She stepped onto the fjord and the water froze solid!
She raced towards the mountains on the other side.

Elsa climbed into the mountains, and with nobody around to worry about, she let all of her power loose for the first time. She felt free! A blizzard flew around her. She even transformed her own dress into a beautiful icy gown.

As she neared the top of the mountain Elsa created a magnificent, shining ice palace. At last, she felt like the person she was always meant to be!

Elsa's blizzard had covered Arendelle with snow and everyone was panicking because it was the middle of summer. Anna knew that she had to find Elsa to thaw out the land – plus, she wanted her big sister back. Now that Elsa's secret was out, they could finally be close again!

Leaving Hans in charge of the kingdom, Anna rode into the mountains. The storm made the journey difficult, though, especially when Anna's horse threw her into the snow. Luckily, she spotted a small building up ahead.

The building was *Wandering Oaken's Trading Post and Sauna*. Anna rushed in and immediately gathered up some supplies.

A young man named Kristoff was also collecting winter supplies. He mentioned that the storm was coming from the North Mountain.

Anna began asking questions. If the storm was on the
North Mountain, Elsa would be there, too!

But Kristoff was busy bargaining for supplies.
Feeling crowded, he finally blurted out, "Now back up,
while I deal with this crook!" The insulted shopkeeper
threw him out empty-handed into the snow.

This gave Anna an idea. She found Kristoff in the stable with his reindeer, Sven, and offered to give him the supplies he needed. In return, she asked that he take her up the North Mountain.

Finally, Kristoff agreed. "We leave at dawn."

"No," said Anna. "We leave right *now*."

Anna and Kristoff climbed
onto a sled and Sven began
pulling them up the mountain.

At first the journey was quite pleasant. Anna told
Kristoff all about Elsa and what had happened
in Arendelle.

But suddenly, a pack of wolves began to chase
them! Anna helped Kristoff to fight off the wolves.
Eventually Sven was forced to leap across a deep
gorge to escape the fierce creatures.

The sled crashed onto the rocks below,
but Anna, Kristoff and Sven were safe.

The trio continued into the forest on foot. They soon came across a beautiful winter scene. Anna was more eager than ever to find Elsa – she had to know more about her sister's amazing power!

"I never knew winter could be so ... beautiful," Anna said.

"But it's so white," added a voice. "How about some colour?"

It was a living snowman!

"I'm Olaf," he said, explaining that Elsa had made him.

Anna gave Olaf a carrot nose, then asked him to lead them to her sister. "We need Elsa to bring back summer."

Olaf grinned. "I've always loved the idea of summer," he said. "The warm sun on my face, getting a gorgeous tan. Just doing whatever snow does in summer."

But Anna and Kristoff were both thinking the same thing: summer would *not* be a good thing for a snowman.

The path up the
mountain grew more
and more difficult.
Luckily, Olaf soon found
a stairway made of ice
leading straight to
Elsa's palace.

"Whoa," exclaimed
Anna in awe, as they
reached the top. The
palace was amazing!

They approached the
front door and Anna
knocked. After a moment,
the door swung open.

Elsa was worried to see Anna. She wanted to return home with her sister, but she knew that everything would be different now that her secret was out. She also remembered how dangerous her powers could be.

"I think you should go, Anna," Elsa said, "I'm sorry. It has to be this way."

But Anna explained that Arendelle was still frozen. If Elsa stayed away, everyone in the kingdom would freeze to death!

Now Elsa was scared. She admitted to Anna
that she didn't know how to undo her magic.

Anna was sure that they could work it out
together, but Elsa thought that was impossible.
It crushed her to know she was still a danger
to others.

Elsa's feelings overwhelmed her until her powers burst out of her – and struck her sister in the heart!

Anna still refused to leave, feeling certain that she could still help her sister. But Elsa insisted – and conjured up a giant snowman to escort Anna outside, along with Kristoff and Olaf.

"Hey, you made me a little brother," Olaf said to Elsa happily. He turned to the huge snowman. "I'm going to name you Marshmallow!"

Elsa ordered Marshmallow to escort Anna and her companions off the mountain. But after Anna hit him with a snowball, he decided to chase them, instead!

The friends ran until they reached a cliff and then lowered themselves down the side. But Marshmallow grabbed the rope and pulled them back up. Anna did the only thing she could think of – she cut the rope!

Luckily, Anna, Kristoff and Olaf landed safely in a soft snowdrift down below. But something was wrong with Anna – her hair was turning white!

"What happened back there? What did she do to you?" Kristoff asked.

Anna explained that Elsa had struck her with her powers.

Kristoff knew just what to do. He had some friends who were experts at just about everything. They could help Anna!

Night fell as Kristoff led Anna and Olaf to the realm of the trolls. Seeing Kristoff, the trolls came out of hiding. Kristoff had spent a lot of time with them as he grew up, so he was practically family!

When an old troll touched Anna's hair, he understood immediately that she had been hurt. "There is ice in your heart, put there by your sister," the old troll said. He explained that Anna would freeze to solid ice forever in one day's time unless the magic was reversed. "Only an act of true love can thaw a frozen heart."

Thinking quickly, Olaf and Kristoff decided to take Anna back home. Surely, Prince Hans could break the spell with a true love's kiss.

Back in Arendelle, Hans had become worried when Anna's horse had returned without her. So he had gathered volunteers to help him find Anna.

When Hans's group arrived at the ice palace, Elsa tried to protect herself. But in the struggle, she was hit by falling ice and knocked out. She ended up being taken back to Arendelle as a prisoner.

Kristoff and Anna were unaware of what had happened at Elsa's ice palace. Kristoff took Anna to the castle gates at Arendelle and sadly passed her over to the servants.

He was starting to realize that he cared deeply about Anna. But he knew she was in grave danger ... and that her true love, Hans, would be able to make her well again.

The servants built a fire in the library to warm Anna, but still she was getting colder by the minute.

Anna was so glad when Hans arrived. She explained what Elsa's icy blast had done and how a true love's kiss could cure her. "Only an act of true love can save me," she said.

But Hans made no move to kiss her. "Could it be this easy?" he asked, his smile turning into a sneer.

Then Hans put out the fire with a jug of water. He explained that he had only been pretending to be in love with her so that he could rule Arendelle!

With Anna nearly frozen, Hans saw that his dream was within reach. All he had to do now was get rid of Elsa.

"You can't," Anna gasped. She collapsed to the floor as the ice slowly spread through her body.

Meanwhile, imprisoned in the castle dungeon, all Elsa could think about was getting away from the kingdom, to protect everyone from her powers. She was also worried about Anna – she didn't know that Anna was back in Arendelle, too.

Elsa became so upset that she lost control of her magic and froze the dungeon. The ice broke her chains and she escaped!

At that same moment, Olaf helped Anna to get to her feet and come outside. The little snowman had realized that Kristoff loved Anna – and that his kiss could save her!

Anna spotted Kristoff running over to her and she began to move slowly towards him, almost completely frozen. But then, she saw something else – Hans was about to strike Elsa with his sword!

With all of her remaining strength, Anna threw herself in front of Elsa. Hans's sword came down just as Anna's body froze to solid ice. With a loud CLANK, the blade shattered.

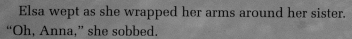

Elsa wept as she wrapped her arms around her sister. "Oh, Anna," she sobbed.

A moment passed. Then something amazing happened. Anna began to thaw! "Elsa?" she whispered.

"You sacrificed yourself for me?" Elsa asked. Anna nodded weakly.

"An act of true love will thaw a frozen heart," Olaf said.

With her sacrifice, Anna had helped Elsa to see
that love was more powerful than fear.

Suddenly, Elsa realized that love was the force that could
control her powers. She raised her arms and the ice and snow
that covered Arendelle melted away.

But Olaf was melting, too! Elsa quickly made a little snow
cloud just for him.

"This is the best day of my life!" he said.

With summer restored, the visiting ships sailed away and Arendelle returned to normal.

Anna replaced Kristoff's sled and his supplies. But he wasn't anxious to leave – especially when Anna surprised him with a kiss!

Elsa created an
ice-skating rink in the castle
and threw open the gates of the
kingdom – she never planned to close
them again.

Everyone had a wonderful time skating with
Queen Elsa and Princess Anna. The kingdom of
Arendelle was a happy place once more!

Anna and Elsa knew that
they would never let anything
come between them again.